Before reading

Look at the book cover
Ask, "What do you thin[k]

Turn to the **Key Words**
the child. Draw their at
the tall letters and thos

During reading

Offer plenty of support and praise as the child reads the story. Listen carefully and respond to events in the text.

When a **Key Word** is used for the first time, it is also shown at the bottom of the page. If the child hesitates over a word, point to the **New Key Words** box and practise reading it together. If the word is phonically decodable, you can sound out the letters and blend the sounds to read the word ("d-o-g, dog"). Praise the child for their effort, then return to the story.

Pause every few pages and ask questions to check the child's understanding of what they have read. If they begin to lose concentration, stop reading and save the page for later.

Celebrate the child's achievement and come back to the story the next day.

After reading

After reading this book, ask, "Did you enjoy the story? What did you like about it?" Encourage the child to share their opinions.

Use the comprehension questions on page 54 to check the child's understanding and recall of the text.

Ladybird

Series Consultant: Professor David Waugh
With thanks to Kulwinder Maude

LADYBIRD BOOKS

UK | USA | Canada | Ireland | Australia
India | New Zealand | South Africa

Ladybird Books is part of the Penguin Random House group of companies
whose addresses can be found at global.penguinrandomhouse.com.
www.penguin.co.uk   www.puffin.co.uk   www.ladybird.co.uk

Penguin
Random House
UK

Original edition of Key Words with Peter and Jane first published by Ladybird Books Ltd 1964
Series updated 2023
This book first published 2023
001

Text copyright © Ladybird Books Ltd, 1964, 2023
Illustrations by Flora Aranyi
Based on characters and design by Gustavo Mazali
Illustrations copyright © Ladybird Books Ltd, 2023

With thanks to Liz Pemberton for her contributions in advising on the illustrations
With thanks to Inclusive Minds for connecting us with their Inclusion Ambassador network,
and in particular thanks to Guntaas Kaur Chugh for her input on the illustrations

Printed in China

The authorized representative in the EEA is Penguin Random House Ireland,
Morrison Chambers, 32 Nassau Street, Dublin D02 YH68

A CIP catalogue record for this book is available from the British Library

ISBN: 978-0-241-51094-0

All correspondence to:
Ladybird Books
Penguin Random House Children's
One Embassy Gardens, 8 Viaduct Gardens, London SW11 7BW

MIX
Paper from
responsible sources
FSC® C018179

Key Words

with Peter and Jane

8a

Granny's birthday

Based on the original
Key Words with Peter and Jane
reading scheme and research by William Murray

Original edition written by William Murray
This edition written by Shari Last
Illustrated by Flora Aranyi
Based on characters and design by Gustavo Mazali

Key Words

am   away   baby

because   been   before

birthday   clothes   day

door   draw   every

find   first   football

garden   gave   if

live   many   next

old   party   pool

round   surprise   three

time   today   very

when   year   your

baby

birthday

clothes

door

draw

football

garden

party

pool

round

three

It was the weekend. Peter was at Pippa's farm with Jane.

"Pippa, your farm is the best!" he said. "There are so many animals to look after."

Pippa helped her mum and dad on the farm every day, and Peter and Jane liked to help Pippa.

Pippa had a surprise for Peter and Jane.

"Look!" said Pippa. "We have three horses now."

Peter and Jane had been to Pippa's farm before. They knew all the animals on the farm, and now there was one more.

"Hello! I am glad you live here now," Jane said to the horse.

"This is a good surprise!"
said Peter.

The horses started running when
they saw the children.

"The horses know we have
something for them!" Jane said.

The children gave some fruit to the
horses. The big horse wanted his
fruit first.

"We can go and see the sheep now,"
said Pippa. "They are round here."

Peter and Jane saw so many sheep.

"Look! Some baby sheep," said Peter.
"They're very sweet."

"How many baby sheep have been
born so far this year, Pippa?"
asked Jane.

"Three," said Pippa.

New Key Words

round   baby   very   year

"Can we find the cows next?"
said Jane.

"Yes, if you like," said Pippa.
"They are round here."

"The cows smell very bad,"
said Peter.

"They have been in the mud,"
said Pippa. "My dad will clean
the mud away next."

"Look! There's a baby cow,"
said Jane.

New Key Words

find   next   if   away

17

It was time to go.

"Today was fun, Pippa," said Peter. "I liked the baby sheep the best."

"Yes, thank you, Pippa," said Jane. "We had a very good time. Next time, you must come and play in our garden."

"Thank you," said Pippa. "I will come round to your house next time and see the rabbits."

New Key Words

time   today   garden

At home, it was time to help Mum and Dad with the gardening. Peter and Jane put on some old clothes.

In the garden, Jane was surprised when her friend Will said, "Jane!"

Will was in his garden with his sister Amber.

"Can you and Peter come round and play?" asked Will.

"Yes, come and play in our garden!" said Amber.

Peter and Jane played football in Will and Amber's garden.

Will and Amber's baby sister, Maya, sat next to the door.

"I am going to draw a picture," she said to Jane.

"You are good at drawing, Maya," said Jane.

"I am drawing our cat and our rabbits," Maya said.

New Key Words

football   door   draw

23

After the game of football, Will and Amber's mum, Cass, gave the children water to drink.

"Thank you," said the older children.

"Thank you, Mum," said Maya.

"Maya is a very good baby," said Jane.

"I'm not a baby!" said Maya. "I am three years old. My doll is a baby."

New Key Words

"Playing football in the hot sun is hard work!" said Will. "Let's go in the little pool next."

They filled a round pool in the garden with water.

The children splashed in the pool in their clothes. Soon, they had cooled down again.

"I like splishing and splashing in the pool!" Maya said.

New Key Words

pool

27

"It's good living next door to you," Peter said to Amber. "We can play football in your garden and jump in your pool. Next time, can you come round to our garden? You can play in our little pool!"

"Yes!" said Amber. "I like your garden because you have a tree house. Let's find a game to play in your garden next time."

The next day was Granny's birthday.

"Surprise!" said Peter and Jane when they saw Granny. "Today is your birthday!"

Granny was very pleased to see them all and so was Grandad.

"This is a good birthday surprise!" said Granny.

New Key Words

birthday

Peter gave Granny a gift for her birthday.

"Thank you, Peter," said Granny. "But I am a bit old for birthdays! I have had so many of them."

"But you must have gifts, Granny!" said Peter.

"We have three birthday gifts for you, Granny," said Jane. "This one is from me."

Next, Mum and Dad gave Granny a gift.

Grandad had a game for Peter and Jane.

"Look at this! I have been drawing a map for you," Grandad said. "You must find three surprises in the garden."

Grandad gave Peter and Jane the map. "Find the first surprise," he said. "After that, find the next one."

"I will be very glad if we find the surprises!" said Peter.

After looking at the map, Peter and Jane walked round the garden. They saw many pots and a very old bench on the map.

"Here are the pots!" said Jane. She looked in every pot.

"It's the first surprise!" Jane said.

"A toy car!" said Peter. "It looks very old. Grandad must have played with it when he was a boy."

New Key Words

"Where will we find the next one?" asked Jane.

Peter looked at the map. "If we go round here," he said, "we will find the next surprise."

They walked round the shed. A box was sitting near the very old bench.

"It's a football!" said Jane.

"First a toy car and now a football. What surprise will we find next?" asked Peter.

The children walked round a big tree and saw a very little door.

"The surprise is here!" said Peter.

"I have not seen a door like this before," said Jane.

"Who lives here?" said Peter.

Peter pulled the door, and the children had a very big surprise.

"Look!" said Peter. "Three toy animals live here! They have little party hats on."

"It's a very little birthday party!" said Jane.

Grandad was pleased that the children liked his surprise. He had been making the little door and the very little birthday party for many weeks.

Next, the children worked very hard to make birthday cards for Granny.

"I am drawing the very little door in the tree," said Peter.

"I am drawing the three toy animals at the very little birthday party!" said Jane.

Granny liked her birthday cards. She gave the children a hug.

"When you go home, I will look at them every day," she said.

New Key Words

"It's time to go, children," said Mum.
"Before it gets dark."

"Thank you, Granny and Grandad!"
said the children.

"Can we have a party for Granny
every weekend?" asked Peter.

"Yes, please!" said Granny.

"And can we see the little door when
we come next time?" asked Jane.

"Yes," said Grandad. "Every time
you come here, your little door
will be waiting."

New Key Words

47

At home, Mum and Dad gave the children some tea.

"That was the best weekend," said Jane, "because we spent time with so many friends."

"It was very good," said Peter. "I liked it because I saw baby animals at the farm."

"I liked it when Grandad gave us a map to find three surprises," said Jane.

"It's time for bed now," said Dad.

Peter and Jane picked up all
their clothes, toys, footballs
and drawings, and they put
everything away.

"Next year, for Granny's birthday
party, I will draw her a card
again," said Peter.

"And I will give Grandad a surprise
for his next birthday," said Jane.
"I will make a little key for the
little door."

51

"Can we read a book before we go to sleep?" Peter asked Mum.

"Yes," said Mum. "Let's read it in Jane's bed today."

"Granny gave me this book when it was my birthday," said Peter.

Mum read the book to Jane and Peter, and very soon the children fell asleep.

New Key Words

53

Questions

Answer these questions about
the story.

1 How many baby sheep have been
born on Pippa's farm?

2 What three things do Peter and
Jane do in Will and Amber's garden?

3 Why does Amber like Peter and
Jane's garden?

4 Why does Grandad give Peter and
Jane a map?

5 What surprise do Peter and Jane
find in the tree?

Before reading

Look at the book cover t
Ask, "What do you think

Turn to the **Key Words** or
the child. Draw their atte
the tall letters and those that have a tail.

During reading

Offer plenty of support and praise as the child reads the story. Listen carefully and respond to events in the text.

When a **Key Word** is used for the first time, it is also shown at the bottom of the page. If the child hesitates over a word, point to the **New Key Words** box and practise reading it together. If the word is phonically decodable, you can sound out the letters and blend the sounds to read the word ("d-o-g, dog"). Praise the child for their effort, then return to the story.

Pause every few pages and ask questions to check the child's understanding of what they have read. If they begin to lose concentration, stop reading and save the page for later.

Celebrate the child's achievement and come back to the story the next day.

After reading

After reading this book, ask, "Did you enjoy the story? What did you like about it?" Encourage the child to share their opinions.

Use the comprehension questions on page 54 to check the child's understanding and recall of the text.

Ladybird

Series Consultant: Professor David Waugh
With thanks to Kulwinder Maude

LADYBIRD BOOKS

UK | USA | Canada | Ireland | Australia
India | New Zealand | South Africa

Ladybird Books is part of the Penguin Random House group of companies
whose addresses can be found at global.penguinrandomhouse.com.
www.penguin.co.uk   www.puffin.co.uk   www.ladybird.co.uk

Original edition of Key Words with Peter and Jane first published by Ladybird Books Ltd 1964
Series updated 2023
This book first published 2023
001

With thanks to Liz Pemberton for her contributions in advising on the illustrations
With thanks to Inclusive Minds for connecting us with their Inclusion Ambassador network,
and in particular thanks to Guntaas Kaur Chugh for her input on the illustrations

Printed in China

The authorized representative in the EEA is Penguin Random House Ireland,
Morrison Chambers, 32 Nassau Street, Dublin D02 YH68

A CIP catalogue record for this book is available from the British Library

ISBN: 978-0-241-51103-9

All correspondence to:
Ladybird Books
Penguin Random House Children's
One Embassy Gardens, 8 Viaduct Gardens, London SW11 7BW

Key Words

with Peter and Jane

11a

Aunt Liz's lost ring

Based on the original
Key Words with Peter and Jane
reading scheme and research by William Murray

Original edition written by William Murray
This edition written by Abbie Rushton
Illustrated by Martyn Cain
Based on characters and design by Gustavo Mazali

Key Words

adventure   around   came

country   cried   everyone   food

fox   idea   last   listen   long

lost   made   man   mouse   name

need   night   nothing   oh   only

plant   police   rain   ran   shout

sky   small   suddenly   through

took   two   use   vet   watch

went   while   woman   world

country

food

fox

man

mouse

night

plant

police

rain

sky

vet

woman

world

Peter, Jane, Mum and Dad had driven to Aunt Liz and Uncle Jack's house.

"Everyone out!" said Dad.

Mum and Dad got the bags out of the car, and Jane rang the doorbell.

Aunt Liz came to the door and laughed when she saw their bags. "I thought you were only coming for two nights!" she said.

"We've packed for sun and rain!" said Mum.

New Key Words

everyone	came	only	two
	night	rain	

"Come in!" said Uncle Jack. "When did you last come here? It's been a while. We've painted the small bedroom now."

"Wow!" said Peter. "Can we see it?"

When the children saw their bedroom, they gasped. The walls looked like the night sky.

"What a great idea!" Jane said.

"It only took us two days," Uncle Jack said.

New Key Words

last	while	small	sky
	idea	took	

"Time for food!" Aunt Liz told everyone.

"Yes!" said Peter. "I only had a small breakfast."

"I made dinner using food I grew at my new allotment," said Aunt Liz, as everyone sat down.

"The allotment!" Peter yelled. "We have a present for you, Aunt Liz."

Peter left the room and came back with a small plant. "It's a strawberry plant," he said.

"I love these! Thank you, Peter," said Aunt Liz.

"Your Aunt Liz has made two new friends at the allotment," said Uncle Jack.

"Yes, their names are Imran and Zara," said Aunt Liz. "Imran is a vet."

New Key Words

food	made	use	plant
	name	vet	

13

"Can we have an adventure at your allotment this weekend?" Jane asked.

"Only if you'll help me to plant my new strawberry plant," said Aunt Liz.

"I need to go for a long run on the beach one day too," said Peter. "I'm doing a fun run in the country soon so I can raise money."

"Oh, great idea!" said Uncle Jack. "What's it for?"

"An animal shelter. They need money for the animals' food," said Peter.

"I love animals," said Jane. "I want to be a vet like your friend Imran."

"I want to work for the police," Peter said.

New Key Words

adventure	need	long
country	oh	police

14

After dinner, Peter showed everyone his new book.

"It's a spotter's book. You have to go on adventures and spot animals," he said.

"We looked for a fox and a mouse in the countryside before we came," said Jane.

Mum checked her watch. "Right, you two, it's time for bed," she said.

As Peter and Jane headed to bed, suddenly everyone heard a CRASH!

"What in the world was that?" Mum said.

"Should we call the police?" Peter asked.

"Let's wait while someone checks outside," Mum said. "There's nothing to be afraid of."

New Key Words

fox	mouse	watch	suddenly
	world	nothing	

Everyone waited by the back door while Aunt Liz went out into the rainy night. They listened for a long time. There was nothing. Then, suddenly, they heard another bang.

"What's going on?" Jane cried.

"It was two small foxes," shouted Aunt Liz. "They came to look through the food bin, but they ran away when they saw me."

At long last, Aunt Liz came in from the rain.

"You two go to bed now," Uncle Jack said. "You need your sleep."

New Key Words

went	listen	cried	shout
	through	ran	

"Please can I stay up a while to watch out for the foxes?" Peter asked.

"Oh, all right, but not for long," said Mum.

"No more adventures for me tonight!" said Jane, yawning. "Night, night, everyone."

As the rain came down, Peter listened hard and watched. He made no sound. Suddenly, a fox crept out of the darkness.

"Wow!" Peter said. He watched the fox for a while. Then, the fox took off into the night. Peter proudly ticked off 'fox' in his book.

New Key Words

"The rain has gone!" said Peter, the next day.

Aunt Liz took Peter and Jane to her allotment and named all the plants.

"Jane, can you pick a few tomatoes?" Aunt Liz said. "You can have a small one if you like."

"You grow the best tomatoes in the world!" said Jane.

Aunt Liz laughed. "I think it will rain again soon," she said, looking at the sky. "Peter, can you go around and put out buckets to collect the rainwater? I can use it to water the plants another day. My plants need lots of water."

New Key Words

around

23

Peter and Jane found a trowel to dig up weeds. "Watch me, then you can use it," said Aunt Liz.

Suddenly, a woman and a man came over. "Liz!" the woman shouted.

Looking around, Aunt Liz said, "Oh, it's Imran and Zara."

"Look at these long leeks!" Imran cried. "Do you need some for the cafe?"

"Oh, wow! I do need some, thanks," Aunt Liz said. "I've got a great idea for a new dish."

New Key Words

woman   man

"Would you like some carrots?" Aunt Liz asked Imran and Zara.

"Oh, you should use them to make your carrot cake, Liz – it's out of this world!" Zara said.

"Aunt Liz, can we make a carrot cake for everyone?" asked Jane.

"Good idea, Jane! Shall we meet you on the beach tomorrow for some cake?" Aunt Liz asked Imran and Zara.

"That would be lovely," Zara said. "Let's hope there's no rain."

New Key Words

At home, Aunt Liz and the children made carrot cake.

"This was such a great idea, Jane," Aunt Liz said. "Nothing makes me happier than baking."

"You said you want to work for the police, Peter, but perhaps you should be a baker," said Mum.

"Oh, maybe!" said Peter.

"I think you'd make a great baker, Peter," said Aunt Liz. "Only, you might need to work on your cleaning skills . . ."

New Key Words

The next morning, everyone went to the beach. Peter went through his spotter's book while they waited for Imran and Zara.

"There's a seagull!" he cried. "But I still need to find a mouse."

"You might see a mouse around at night," Jane said.

They saw a man and a woman walking over to them. Peter said, "There's Imran and Zara!"

Peter ran to meet them.

"I need to train for my fun run!" he shouted back to Mum.

Tess and Kit ran after him.

New Key Words

31

Aunt Liz was looking around some rock pools. Jane went to join her.

"That's a nice bit of driftwood," Aunt Liz said. "We could use it to make an insect house."

"Good idea!" said Jane. "We saw this in Peter's book."

Jane and Aunt Liz went to pick up the driftwood, but it was too big.

"Oh, there's a smaller bit," Jane said, pointing to a bit that was floating in the water.

New Key Words

Aunt Liz pulled the driftwood out of the water. "Let's use that bit," she said.

"Now, I need to find a crab for Peter," said Jane, looking around at the rock pools. "There's a crab in his book."

"Oh no!" Aunt Liz suddenly shouted.

"What's the matter?" Jane asked.

"My ring! Oh, I've lost my ring!" cried Aunt Liz.

New Key Words

lost

Peter ran to Aunt Liz and Jane. "What's happened?" he asked.

"Aunt Liz has lost her ring," Jane said.

"I think it's lost for good," Aunt Liz cried. "We can't look through all these rock pools."

"I've got an idea!" Peter said. "We need to go back to where you last walked. That's how the police look for things."

Aunt Liz and Jane took Peter back to where they found the driftwood. They looked all around, but there was nothing.

New Key Words

They went back to tell everyone what had happened.

"Maybe someone will hand the ring in to the police," said Dad.

"Let's look around there again, Policeman Peter," said Uncle Jack. "I'll race you!"

Peter and Uncle Jack ran back to the rock pools while the others had some of Aunt Liz's cake.

Aunt Liz looked sad and said nothing. She watched Uncle Jack and Peter looking around for her lost ring.

New Key Words

"Imran, do you like being a vet?" Jane asked. "I like the idea of being a vet one day."

"Oh, yes!" said Imran. "That's a great idea. There's nothing in the world like being a vet. The training took a long time, but I loved it."

Peter ran back from the rock pools. "Dad, will you use your watch to time me while I run?" he said.

Everyone watched while Peter ran to the sea and back. The two dogs ran after him.

"You beat your last time by two seconds," Dad said. "Great job!"

New Key Words

41

After leaving Imran and Zara at the beach, everyone went back to Aunt Liz and Uncle Jack's garden.

"It may rain soon," said Uncle Jack, looking at the sky.

"Let's make our insect house before the rain comes," said Aunt Liz. "We'll use the driftwood we found at the beach."

As soon as they'd made the insect house, a bee landed on it and went through a gap.

"Oh, look!" cried Peter.

"That bee has a lovely new house!" said Jane, as Peter ticked 'bee' in his book.

New Key Words

The sun was setting and it was just starting to rain when they all went inside.

Peter and Jane helped Dad to pack the car. The family needed to go home after dinner, and it was a long drive.

"Oh, Peter!" cried Jane suddenly. "A mouse! I saw a mouse!"

"Where?" Peter shouted.

"It ran through that gap in the tree," said Jane, but Peter saw nothing.

New Key Words

At last, everyone sat down to dinner. "We've had two great days with fantastic food, Aunt Liz!" said Jane.

"We're glad you came," said Uncle Jack. "It's been –"

He stopped because Kit suddenly ran through the kitchen, barking. Tess quickly ran through after him.

"What in the world . . .?" Mum said.

Aunt Liz went to look. "It's a mouse!" she shouted.

New Key Words

Peter took his spotter's book and ran round the table to look. "It's the mouse Jane saw! If there's a mouse here, I'll find it," he said.

"Peter, you won't find the mouse," Mum said. "It'll have gone through a small hole somewhere."

Peter went under the bench, where the dogs were sniffing around.

"There's nothing," Peter shouted. "Oh!"

Peter suddenly came out. "There's no lost mouse, but here's a lost ring!" he said proudly.

"Oh, Peter!" Aunt Liz cried. "Thank you! Now I remember – I took it off when we were baking."

New Key Words

49

Everyone was very happy that the lost ring had been found.

"All right, everyone, it's time we made our way home," Dad said.

The family went out to their car, and Aunt Liz and Uncle Jack waved them off.

In the car, Jane said, "It's too bad you didn't see a mouse this weekend, Peter."

"Oh well," said Peter. "I did see a fox, seagulls and a bee. *And* I found a lost ring!"

"Yes, and we made a cake and an insect house, and I met a vet," Jane added.

New Key Words

51

The next week, Peter did his fun run in the countryside. Mum, Dad and Jane shouted and cheered for him.

"You ran a long way, Peter!" Mum cried, as he ran over the finish line.

"And everyone gave money for the animal shelter," Dad added.

"Oh, Peter, look through there," Jane suddenly shouted. "Under that bush. Can you see the mouse?"

"Oh, wow! Maybe it came to cheer me on too," said Peter. "Thanks, mouse! I can tick you off in my book now."

New Key Words

Before reading

Look at the book cover tog
Ask, "What do you think wi

To build independence, th
at the start of this book. If
back to pages 6 and 7 in 10a and read the words again with
the child.

During reading

Offer plenty of support and praise as the child reads the story.
Listen carefully and respond to events in the text.

In 10c, the new **Key Words** are not shown at the bottom of
the page. If the child hesitates over a word, turn to the back
of the book to practise reading it together. If the word is
phonically decodable, you can sound out the letters and
blend the sounds to read the word ("d-o-g, dog"). Praise the
child for their effort, then return to the story.

Pause every few pages and ask questions to check the child's
understanding of what they have read. If they begin to lose
concentration, stop reading and save the page for later.

Celebrate the child's achievement and come back to the
story the next day.

After reading

After reading this book, ask, "Did you enjoy the story? What did
you like about it?" Encourage the child to share their opinions.

Use the comprehension questions on page 54 to check the
child's understanding and recall of the text.

Ladybird

Series Consultant: Professor David Waugh
With thanks to Kulwinder Maude

LADYBIRD BOOKS

UK | USA | Canada | Ireland | Australia
India | New Zealand | South Africa

Ladybird Books is part of the Penguin Random House group of companies
whose addresses can be found at global.penguinrandomhouse.com.
www.penguin.co.uk   www.puffin.co.uk   www.ladybird.co.uk

Penguin
Random House
UK

Original edition of Key Words with Peter and Jane first published by Ladybird Books Ltd 1964
Series updated 2023
This book first published 2023
001

Text copyright © Ladybird Books Ltd, 1964, 2023
Illustrations by Pablo Gallego with colour work by Valeria Abatzoglu
Based on characters and design by Gustavo Mazali
Illustrations copyright © Ladybird Books Ltd, 2023

With thanks to Liz Pemberton for her contributions in advising on the illustrations
With thanks to Inclusive Minds for connecting us with their Inclusion Ambassador network,
and in particular thanks to Guntaas Kaur Chugh for her input on the illustrations

Printed in China

The authorized representative in the EEA is Penguin Random House Ireland,
Morrison Chambers, 32 Nassau Street, Dublin D02 YH68

A CIP catalogue record for this book is available from the British Library

ISBN: 978-0-241-51102-2

All correspondence to:
Ladybird Books
Penguin Random House Children's
One Embassy Gardens, 8 Viaduct Gardens, London SW11 7BW

MIX
Paper from
responsible sources
FSC® C018179

Key Words

with Peter and Jane

10c

Save our bookshop!

Based on the original
Key Words with Peter and Jane
reading scheme and research by William Murray

Original edition written by William Murray
This edition written by Ben Hulme-Cross
Illustrated by Pablo Gallego with colour work by Valeria Abatzoglu
Based on characters and design by Gustavo Mazali

It was a snowy morning, and Peter and Jane had just finished breakfast in the kitchen.

"Today's going to be great!" said Peter. "It'll be so much fun to play in the snow at school!"

"Right, Peter and Jane," Mum called from the next room. "Clear up those breakfast things in the kitchen. Put on lots of warm clothes this morning, please. They said on the television there will be even more snow this afternoon."

7

Peter and Jane walked to school in the snow.

"I love snow so much!" said Jane, laughing. "Can we play in the snow this afternoon, then have a fire in the living room and play music?"

"Yes!" Mum said, laughing too. "The snow will still be here. It's stopped snowing this morning, but it's going to snow again this afternoon."

"That's lots of snow," said Peter. "We can make snow people. A snow family!"

They were so happy about the snow that morning that they didn't see the poster in the bookshop right away.

"No!" said Peter and Jane. "The bookshop is going to close!" Their family loved the bookshop. They stopped by the window.

"I thought all the people in town loved the bookshop!" said Mum.

Jane thought it was very sad. She'd been so happy at breakfast. Now, even the snow and the thought of a fire this afternoon didn't make her happy.

11

All morning, Peter and Jane thought about the bookshop closing down. At lunchtime, their friends had a great time playing in the snow. Even when Peter and Jane joined in, they still weren't happy. Then, in the afternoon, it began to snow again.

"Look at those frowns! I thought you'd have a great day," said Mum, after school. "Are you still sad about the bookshop?"

They really were sad.

On the way home, Peter and Jane wanted to stop at the bookshop.

"Yes, let's stop by there," Mum said.

"Why are you closing?" Jane asked the bookseller. "We love this place!"

"Lots of people love the bookshop," the bookseller told them. "But these days, people can buy books in lots of different places – in many different shops and online."

When they got home, Mum said, "I'll light the fire. Then, I thought we could make a family plan to help the bookshop."

"Great, Mum!" said Jane.

Then, Peter and Jane jumped happily out of the snow and sat at the table by the fire.

"Right, let's think," began Jane. "Lots of people still love bookshops, even if they shop online. Why do we like bookshops?"

"Because our family loves books!" said Peter.

17

"Lots of people like books," Mum began, "but we can still buy them online or in bigger shops. Why buy a book in a bookshop?"

"It's good to look at a book before you buy it," said Jane. "You can even go to a bookshop with your family, and it can be a great day out. It makes you feel happy."

"Right then, we must tell people that bookshops make them happy," said Peter.

19

"I've got it!" said Jane. "Let's have a party at the bookshop for people who love books."

"Mr Grant could play some music," said Peter.

"That's a great plan!" Mum told them. "Then people would see how much families and friends love the bookshop."

Mum got up and walked to the kitchen.

"What if we got a story about the party in the newspaper?" said Jane. "Then even more people would hear about it."

Peter thought hard. Then, he had a different plan. "Mum, you know those comic books I love?" he called.

"The ones about the elf town? That writer is great," said Mum, from the kitchen.

"Can we write to him on your computer?" asked Peter. "He's called Doctor Fire."

Mum got her computer and looked online for Doctor Fire. Then, she handed the computer to Peter.

These were the words that Peter wrote:

I love your books so much! They make me and my friends very happy. My family even loves the television show of your books.

We all love our high street bookshop too. It sells lots of different books. This morning, we found out that it is closing.

It would be great if you could write to the people at the bookshop, so they know that lots of people want the bookshop to stay.

Thanks,
Peter and Jane

25

The next afternoon after school, Peter and Jane walked by the bookshop again.

"Right, we've been thinking," Jane told the bookseller. "Lots of our friends like your bookshop, and we'd love it to stay."

"We thought we could have a party with great music and lots of people. What do you think?" said Peter.
"You might even get pictures of the bookshop in the newspaper."

"What a great plan!" said the bookseller.
"We have room for a party. I can
tell people why I love working here.
I'm Priya, by the way, and this is Clive."

"Great to meet you! I'm Jane, and this
is Peter," said Jane. "We'll find a way
to tell lots of people about the party."

The children thought about the party
as they walked home in the snow. By the
time they got back, Jane had an even
better plan to make sure lots of people
would come to the party.

The next morning, Jane said, "No time for breakfast! We've got to get to school."

"Hang on," said Peter. "I want my breakfast!"

At school, Jane told her teacher about the bookshop.

"Mr Bell," Jane began, "we're going to have a reading party to help the bookshop. The children from school could dress up as someone from a book they love. Families could buy books there, then we could all read and play music at the party."

"That's a great plan, Jane!" said Mr Bell.

That afternoon, Jane told Clive her plan.

"The party won't even cost money!" she said. "Children from school will come, then they will see why they should buy books here, as well as online and in other shops."

"We might still have to close," Clive told the family. "But it's a great plan. I like that you thought of having music too."

By the fire at home, Dad helped Peter make a poster on the computer. A film Jane loved was on television.

"This party is going to be so much fun," said Jane. "People love dressing up."

"Stop the film, Jane!" said Peter, with a happy laugh. "Doctor Fire says he talked to the bookshop. He thinks it's great that we want to help!"

The next morning, Mr Bell told Peter he could put the posters up at school.

Peter and Jane were very happy, and their friends thought the reading party would be great fun. They told their friends to tell their families about the party too.

"Just think how happy people will be if they have great new books to read!" said Jane.

That afternoon, Peter and Jane put posters up in lots of different places.

Then, when they got home, Mum told them to come and look at the television. On the television news, there was a story about Peter and Jane's reading party. People even began talking about it online too.

"*You'll* be in the newspaper or on television next!" Dad said, laughing.

On the afternoon of the party, Jane got dressed up as a wolf, and Peter got dressed up as a wizard. By the time they got to the bookshop, it was packed.

One of Peter's posters was in the window, and there were lots of people! Someone was selling hot drinks at a table by the door, and Mr Grant was playing music by the table.

Lots of children were sitting on the floor and at tables in the shop.

All afternoon, people walking by stopped to hear the music and look in the bookshop. Some people wanted to see the children dressed up, and many people wanted to buy books.

The booksellers were very happy. "I never thought so many people would come!" Clive said.

Peter and Jane were very happy too.

43

Then, Peter began yawning. They had been reading for some time, and it was getting dark.

"Maybe we should stop now," said Jane. "You look even more tired than me."

"No," said Peter. "People are still buying books. We can't stop!"

"You're right," said Jane. "Look, there are even more people here now than there were this afternoon."

"Right, children!" began Priya, the bookseller. "You've been so much help. We've been selling books all afternoon, and lots of people said they would come back again. We think the shop will not have to close down after all!"

The people in the shop cheered.

"Now," said Priya, "there is someone here who would like to talk to you."

Someone was coming in the door . . .

It was Doctor Fire!

The children were very happy. Someone from the newspaper was there. There was even someone filming for television!

When the room was still, Doctor Fire began to talk.

"I'm here because of Peter and Jane," he said. "They wrote to me and asked me to visit the bookshop."

49

"I love bookshops," Doctor Fire told them. "When I was a boy, I would go to my town's bookshop with my dad. I looked at all those different books on the tables and thought, 'Maybe one day I'll be a writer.'

"Now, I live by this bookshop, and I don't want it to close. Look at all these children reading. Look at all these people who have come to buy books this afternoon."

After speaking to the people in the bookshop, Doctor Fire talked to Peter and Jane.

"You did a great thing here," he told them.

The television people filmed Peter and Jane talking to Doctor Fire. Then, the television reporter asked Peter and Jane if they had something to say to the people at home.

"Yes," Jane said. "Bookshops are great!"

"Even when it's snowing!" said Peter, with a laugh.